# May There Always Be Sunshine

A traditional song adapted by **Jim Gill**
Illustrated by **Susie Signorino-Richards**

For information regarding Jim's music and books for children,
contact Jim Gill Inc., PO Box 2263, Oak Park, IL 60303-2263 or
www.jimgill.com.

Library of Congress Card Catalog Number 2001126097
ISBN 0-9679038-6-6

Original oil paintings by Susie Signorino-Richards
Art direction and design by Sheila Sachs

Printed in the United States of America
First edition, October 2001; Second pressing November 2002

**I** have sung this Russian folk song in schools, libraries, and church basements with thousands of children and their parents. After singing the first four lines of the song, children share their ideas of what they would like there to always be. Everyone sings along as we create a new song. I have kept a list of hundreds of the children's ideas over the years. This book contains just a few.

My wife, friends, and I created this book with the hope that parents and teachers might help young children create their own books based on this simple and beautiful song. Children will be happy to tell you all of the things that they would like there to always be. After that it only takes some paper, crayons and a bit of time.

Educators say that writing experiences such as these are key to a child's grasp of the complexities of literacy.

I believe such experiences teach an even more important lesson. Each person's thoughts and ideas are worthy of our attention—and only get better with exercise. The joy of life is in **thinking**, **creating** and **doing**.

Jim Gill

May there always be sunshine.

May there always be blue skies.

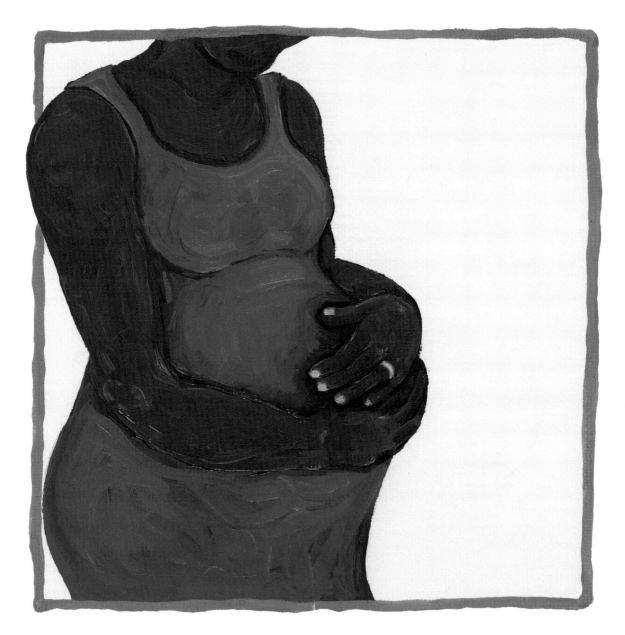

May there always be Mama.

May there always be me.

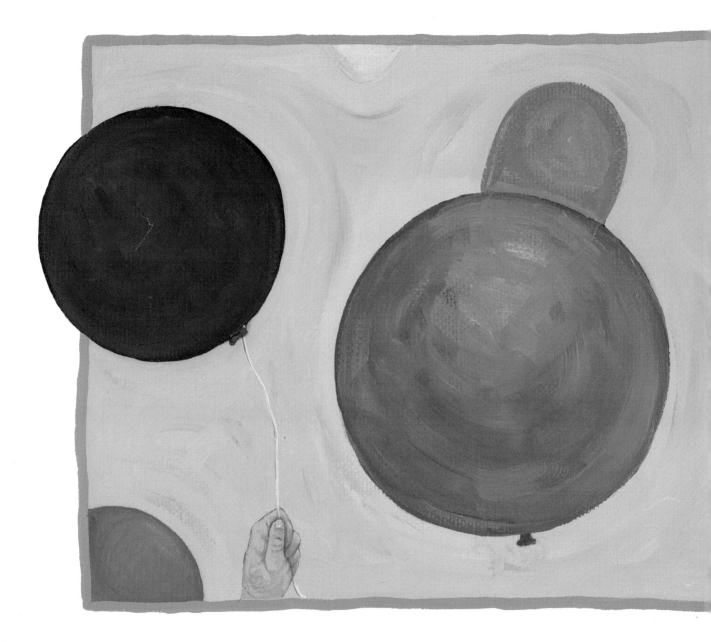

May there always be colors.

May there always be grapes.

May there always be teeth.

May there always be fish.

May there always be pancakes.

May there always be books.

May there always be blankets.

May there always be dads.

May there always be farmers.

May there always be hats.

May there always be dancing.

May there always be rain.

May there always be skyscrapers.

May there always be fiddles.

May there always be birthdays.

May there always be us.

And may there always be: lightning · Kentucky · cheese · apple juice · guitars · horses · ducks · bicycles · firemen · bumper cars · basketball · hamburgers · pets · candy · chocolate · school · children · swimming pools · trucks · church · balloons · apple pie · underwear · dinosaurs · chickens · flowers · matzo ball soup · fun · cars · sisters · friends · cheetahs · Christmas · food · slides · singing · snow · teachers · pop · Valentine's Day · shoes · rainbows · gardens · oranges · dogs · families · nighttime · toy stores · chairs · fans · lakes · happiness · computers · alligators · everything · brothers · spaghetti · libraries · Hanukkah · cats · cake · grandpas · soccer · love · popcorn · baseball · zucchini · music · piñatas · airplanes · games · robots · Pez · beds · buses · oceans · grandmas · hair · hot dogs · toys · carrots · grass · strawberry pie · puddles · presents · corn · riddles · morning · vacations · cookies · seashells · clouds · bubblebath · crayons · windows · swings · animals · God · pizza · skirts · paint · tractors · rock and roll · Easter eggs · clowns · the gym · houses · babies · cousins · museums · playing · stereos · potato chips · bubbles · puzzles · zebras · pumpkins · roller coasters · hopscotch · jumping · farms · smiles · mail · movies · names · hot air balloons · fireworks · goats · bears · haircuts · glasses · light bulbs · 7-Up · coats · merry-go-rounds · backyards · fruit · the Pepsi truck · Elvis · words · hot soup · Santa Claus · jokes · leaves · apple trees · giraffes · buildings · canoes · witches · hearts · turkeys · snowmen · monkeys · sprinklers · T-shirts · dolphins · playgrounds · lasagna · orange juice · doctors · peacocks · gymnastics · candles · trampolines · noses · magnets · trees · ornaments · ghosts · water · monster trucks · pencils · Kool-Aid · tomatoes · storms · blueberries · penguins · angels · stop signs · chocolate chip cookies · cards · comics · the world · planets · magic · drums · nature · sailboats · bouncing · restaurants · cartoons · scissors · pillows · stars · weights · Band-Aids · butterflies · the circus · all of things